CAPE HATTERAS LIGHT STATION

JUL 1 8 2017

BUXTON, NORTH CAROLINA

My Rainy Day Cat

By Kevin McCabe • Illustrated by Kim Mosher

Fur Cat Press

My Rainy Day Cat

Written by Kevin McCabe and Illustrated by Kim Mosher

Published in 2015 by Kevin McCabe-Fur Cat Press

P.O. Box 743, Buxton, NC 27920, www.kimmosherdesigns.com

ISBN 978-0-692-42559-6

Second Edition

Fur Cat Press

Made in U.S.A.

Special Thanks to Jones Printing, Charles Jones & John Keep

Introduction

There's an echoing rumble in the distant ocean as the sky darkens. However, our beautiful home is tucked deep within the maritime forest next to the Cape Hatteras Lighthouse and we are all safe. The first big drops of rain are dancing on the pond and quickly coming towards the house. We hear the welcomed rain hit the leaves of our favorite trees as it taps on the roof above. The rain is here. Suddenly there's a flash and our cat runs across the lawn like a cheetah on the great African veldt to a waiting open door. His fate has been sealed for the rest of this wet gray day. I wish we could all be as lucky as my rainy day cat.

The poem "My Rainy Day Cat" was actually written as a thank you gift to my mother. She loved animals and gave generously to several organizations that help them. A lost dog or a stray cat could always find dinner at my mother's house.
Years ago she learned that our old cat BK needed a very expensive oral surgery. Times were tight back then and sadly we could not afford to have the procedure done. Within a day a check appeared in the mail from my mother. BK the cat lived another seven years and taught everyone a valuable lesson about life, living, and giving.

I always enjoyed writing and the words to this poem were found rather quickly. I remember looking out the window on a rainy day scribbling down what I saw including the tail of my cat sleeping under my bed. Writing what your eyes see may be easier than drawing it. My wife the artist would prove this point when we decided to turn the poem into a book with her imagination and illustrations reflecting the words.

I met Kim in May 1985 while she was vacationing in Hatteras, NC at the old Durant Station with her VCU photography professors. We were destined to meet at the Lighthouse beach where I happened to be surfing. Shortly after, she moved down permanently to pursue her art and love of nature. Kim's photography was wonderful but she was always an artist to me.
Her colorful sketches and imagination are amusing to the soul. Her artistic mind began to flow while living in the relaxed atmosphere of the island. Beautiful colorful pencil drawings of fish and birds flew and swam from her paper.
Highly detailed images became her trademark with everything drawn entirely by hand!

Kim worked on the illustrations for this book for nearly five years with the Cape Hatteras Lighthouse keeping her company out her studio window. Layers and layers of colored pencil and perhaps miles of lines if all were connected. Look close and you may find hidden animals or designs. Count the leaves on the trees, there are thousands. View each page very slowly to properly understand this magical story. Pretend you are walking the sea-glass beach with the leopard and dream along with "My Rainy Day Cat."

It's a very gray day and the rain does fall,

A little while later I see a cat's paw.

Each raindrop takes him deeper...

deeper into the dream,

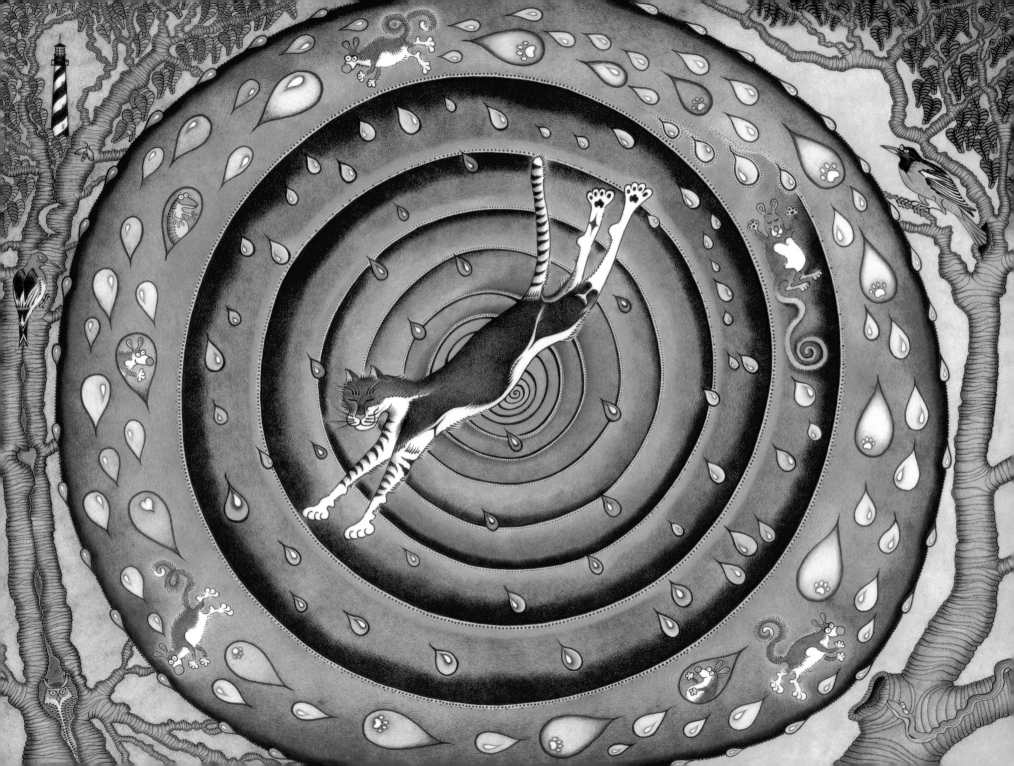

He's now hunting salmon in a wild Alaskan stream.

Wrapped in a ball with his tail over his head,

In reality, he's asleep under my bed.

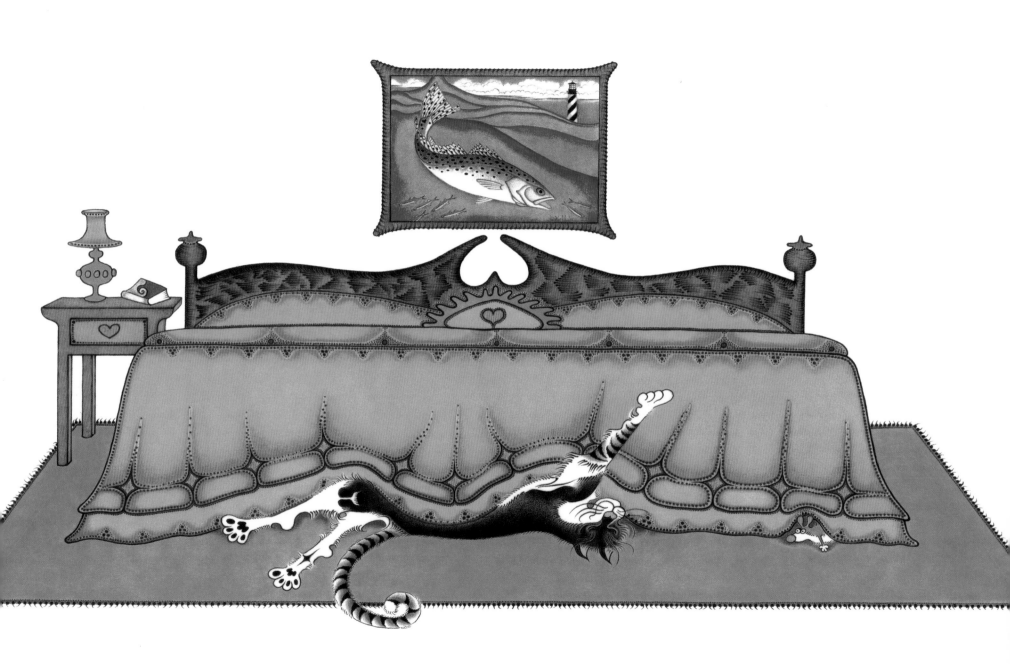

The sky gets darker and the rain does pour,

He's now a leopard walking a distant shore.

People do this and people do that,

But on a rainy day I must have a cat.

My Rainy Day Cat

It's a very gray day and the rain does fall,
A little while later I see a cat's paw.
Each raindrop takes him deeper deeper into the dream
He's now hunting salmon in a wild Alaskan Stream.
Wrapped in a ball with his tail over his head,
In reality, he's asleep under my bed.
The sky gets darker and the rain does pour,
He's now a leopard walking a distant shore.
People do this and people do that,
But on a rainy day, I must have a cat.

By: Kevin Mc Cabe